THUMBING DAYS

NON-FICTION

Paul Perilli

Cyberwit.net
HIG 45 Kaushambi Kunj, Kalindipuram
Allahabad - 211011 (U.P.) India
http://www.cyberwit.net
Tel: +(91) 9415091004
E-mail: info@cyberwit.net

Printed at Repro India Limited.

NOTE: Several of these non-fiction pieces appeared in a slightly different form in the following publications: "Hacker" in *bioStories*, Fall 2014; "Eulogy For the Bomb" in *bioStories*, Fall 2016; "The Solids Truck" in *Blue Collar Review*, Fall 2018; "Word of the Day: Gauche" in *Thema*, March 2018; "Word of the Day: Narcotize" in *The Blotter*, October 2018; "Word of the Day: Gallivantriloquism" in *Redemption* – an anthology published by Charlie Taylor, February 2021.

Contents

THUMBING DAYS

In one of the last scenes of Leonard Gardner's novel *Fat City* Ernie Munger, a lightweight boxer, has just won an undercard match in Salt Lake City he's paid $50 for. To save bus fare back to his home in Stockton Munger decides to thumb. The first man to stop takes him as far as the airport turnoff and on a road at the edge of the city he's picked up by two young women. Along the dark highway the conversation becomes testy and Munger gets into an argument with the driver. It goes on until she stops the car and insists he get out. It's night, in the middle of the desert, and at first Munger resists. But eventually he opens the door, grabs his bag from the back and the women speed off. There are few other cars at that hour so Munger sleeps by the side of the road and isn't picked up until after sunrise.

I was reminded of that scene on a recent nine-day driving vacation in New Mexico, where I saw as many as twenty hitchhikers standing in pebbly breakdown lanes with packs hanging off their shoulders or set down on the pavement next to them, their thumbs held out, their eyes hopeful ours would be the vehicle to give them a lift. I was surprised to see so many in so short a time, more than I'd seen in many years, and I wondered if it was again an acceptable social custom, looked at as an all right way to get from one place to another. Pack a bag, head to the highway and hope to get somewhere with minimum hassle.

As I approached those men of various ages I was inclined to pull over and invite them into the backseat of our rental and take them as far as I could along the route we were traveling: to Las Cruces on our way to White Sands, or to Espanola as we were heading to the mineral springs at Ojo Caliente. Wherever we were going. However we could help.

But inclined is not an action verb unless it's followed through on and by now you already know we didn't stop. Not once did my wife

Geraldine or I ease up on the gas in consideration even if most of those men with suntanned faces and wind-blown hair, wearing short-sleeved shirts and blue jeans, or jerseys and shorts, needy as they appeared, and likely were, seemed harmless enough. Some were surely down on their luck, as that saying goes about folks with little money, not wanting to fork over precious cash for a bus ticket. Though I imagine at least a few must have been out for a bit of adventure, maybe even without a firm destination, with the intention to bust out on their own for a while.

But most of all, when I spotted those men I was reminded of my own thumbing days. I saw my younger, restless self with long black hair and fatigued denim clothing and scuffed orange work boots heading somewhere, anywhere: across town, to visit a friend at a college two states away, once from Boston to Chicago. That was at a time everyone was doing it. So many hitchhikers back then it was, to compare it to an e-business phenomenon, a kind of Uber-like ride sharing system without credit card involvement. It felt like one big mobile community of like-minded folks. Those with vehicles willing to take you along with them. Those without needing to get from here to find out what was there.

In that former time money was never asked for or exchanged. And there were occasions when a car with three or four people in it would roll to a stop and a party atmosphere would be in progress, some music would be playing, Led Zeppelin, Stevie Wonder or Bob Dylan, and my trip, no pun intended, would be enhanced with the proffer of a joint, or one of my gracious hosts would hand a can of beer my way I'd say thanks to before cracking the flip top. I lived by the rule to never refuse anyone's hospitality, though more often than not conversation alone was shared instead of the resources to get me high. Whatever. I enjoyed those interactions, of meeting people I didn't know and likely would never see again. Of being exposed to all those other lives and finding out they weren't that much different from me.

A check of Wikipedia's hitching examples include Douglas Adams' interstellar hitchhiking in *The Hitchhiker's Guide to the Galaxy* and

Robert Heinlein's inter-dimensional hitchhiking in *Job: A Comedy of Justice*. From the ages of 14 to 23 I, of course, was involved in that activity's earthly form, a land-based itinerant of sorts, without a car or much money but always on the move.

This many years later it's still easy to recall some of those experiences. The buzzed-up truck driver who had stopped for a friend and I on Route 2 in western Massachusetts and who, learning we had graduated from college a month earlier, told us the key to being successful was "having good bullshit." "You gotta have good *buulllllshit*," he said with a heavy stress on the first syllable. He repeated it so many times during the hour or so we were in his truck his face and voice remain in my head all these years later. And yes, it was advice I should have taken more seriously.

I haven't forgotten the mellow thirtyish hippie couple who picked me up in northern Vermont on my way back from hiking the Appalachian Trail. Fortunate they were heading to the Boston area as I was, we were halfway there when they asked if I was interested in partying with them that night? From the conversation that had gone on before that, and the looks they were giving each other waiting for my response, I wasn't sure if they were asking me to join them in a threesome or go to a bash with their friends? Whatever their intentions, I declined the offer, feeling pretty sure whichever scenario they had in mind would be enhanced with hallucinogens.

Recently I read about the talking, tweeting, hitchhiking robot named HitchBOT, the creation of Canadian researchers who sent it out on the road by itself hoping the people picking it up would see it safely to its destination. After successful trips through Canada, the Netherlands and Germany, HitchBOT came to the U.S. for a cross-country tour. Starting in Boston, with San Francisco its goal, HitchBOT took in a Red Sox game at Fenway Park, toured midtown Manhattan and made it as far as Philadelphia, where it was vandalized beyond repair, its arms torn off, its head gone missing. In spite of that brutal encounter, HitchBOT's final tweet remained upbeat: "My trip must come to an end for now, but my love for humans will never fade."

As HitchBOT's creators surely knew, danger must always be on the mind of inanimate as well as human hitchhikers. My personal experiences were not always lively conversations, rock & roll music and a can of beer to drink on the way. There were plenty of disturbing moments too.

On summer vacations in my mid teens I caddied at a private country club ten miles from my house. Twice a day, four or five days a week I was on Route 20 with my thumb out looking for strangers to take me there and back. Parents would never let their kids do that now, and while mine were reluctant, the route was popular with a lot of caddies and more often than not the people stopping knew where I was going. They were friendly, generous, easy to talk to. But being young and alone didn't always attract folks with the best intentions. Several situations came up when I was sure I'd have to defend myself. On one afternoon a man wondered if I wanted to go to his place to check out his collection of *Playboy* magazines? Another guy was more blunt, asking if I wanted to earn ten dollars? Hearing that, my fists tightened and I told him to pull over and let me out. Which he did without the exchange of another word.

I never told my parents about those and other creepy moments I experienced during my three years commuting to the country club. I never doubted I could get out of any trouble that might come up. I started carrying a pocketknife. I was never deterred. In those days hitching seemed as natural as walking down the street.

Two-thirds into that trip from Boston to Chicago I was let off in a bleak area along I-90 just south of Toledo. It was night, spooky, and I was nervous. All kinds of possibilities ran through my brain and none of them were good. My plans hadn't included being dropped off in a desolate stretch of highway at that hour. A sleeping bag was strapped to my backpack but no way I was going to use it. Not there, in the brush, trash, dirt and who knew what else. I wasn't as tough as Ernie Munger.

Speeding cars and semi trailers blew past me. I had to go on though and my thumb was out a half hour only when an off-duty cop pulled up wondering where I was from and just what the hell I was doing out there by myself? Desperate I was, and I pled my innocence and ignorance. Hearing that, he told me to get in and then took me, out of his way I must add, to the Greyhound Station downtown. Before he let me go he made sure to find out I had enough money for a bus ticket and I promised I'd buy one. Instead of that, I slept in a chair with my backpack in my lap. The next morning I was out on I-90 and by mid afternoon I was with my friends in Chicago.

Fortunate I was that night in Toledo to be picked up so quick and experience such generosity. (HitchBOT could have used the same luck in Philly.) But I remain under the impression getting a ride never took very long. Being in the right spot to make it easy for cars to stop was vital to that success. A few steps after a traffic light on a 2 or 4 lane highway. In a breakdown lane not far past the point an on-ramp merged onto an Interstate. A lot of drivers willing to take you on was equally important and they were abundant back when I was hitching.

Then, at some point, my thumbing days ended. I've no recollection of that last ride. It might have been the day before I got my first car, when I made the switch from needing a lift to providing them. And I picked up lots of hitchers. It was a good time to do that. And maybe it's back to being that way?

HACKER

"You take a job you become the job," Wizard said in Martin Scorcese's cult classic *Taxi Driver*.

I felt much like Wizard the summer I was twenty and drove a taxi for Red Cab, a Waltham, MA company owned by my older cousin Joey. Joey was a wise-cracking, street smart, tough guy, who at the same time was incredibly generous and also ambitious. At an early age he turned an interest in cars and a job in a gas station into a business that would grow from owning a few cabs to having a fleet of them and eventually include school buses as well as vans for people with special needs and senior citizens, making make him millions of dollars.

Of course, I made a bit less than that working for him those months, an amount that fluctuated depending on how many hours I was willing to put in. And that was a lot. I was hired to drive weekdays but if there was a no-show or someone was late or quit, and that happened often enough, I would volunteer to stay on. I could drive long hours, 12 or 16 of them with only a few breaks: a to-go breakfast from Wilson's Diner, a couple of takeout slices from Piece o' Pizza, a large afternoon coffee from Tony's Spa. I liked the money and it was there to make if I wanted it, and there were times I'd be home with my family or shooting hoop with friends thinking I could, and probably should, be on the road making some cash instead. I took the job, I became the job.

It wasn't more than a few days after I started that my friends began calling me Hacker, as in "Hey Hacker, you coming out with us tonight?" It was a moniker I couldn't dissuade them from using. The identifier, I was sure, would turn off the females we ran into at parties or bars or the beach and doom me to a long dry summer. But, to my surprise, it actually turned out to be a good conversation starter, and I recall more than a few wide-eyed faces exclaiming, "Wow, are you really doing that?" My answer in the affirmative would lead to the usual follow up questions. "Is it interesting?" "It can be." "Are the people weird?" "Mostly." "Do they give you great tips?" "Not especially."

In truth, I picked up the whole gamut of local humanity and folks passing through Waltham for whatever reason. I transported executives to and from the technology companies out on Fourth Ave, Bear Hill Road and Winter Street to Logan Airport. I took bossy old ladies who gave me ten cent tips to Super Market to do their grocery shopping. An hour later I might pick them up again and for another ten cents carry half a dozen bags to their door and maybe even respond to a command issued with the authority of a drill sergeant: "Don't just leave them there, take them inside." I drove men to their jobs in the mornings and picked up others outside bars in the evenings and nights, and who, shitfaced and disoriented, might be overcome with a swell of generosity that could yield a fifty percent tip I'd have no problem pocketing. I took people of all ages to Waltham Hospital for tests or admission or to visit an ill spouse or child. Some would go into great detail about their plight and the fear I heard resonating in their voices might depress me until my next pickup occupied the back seat and a new conversation started up. There were times, once a day maybe, when I'd turn the meter off early to keep the fare low for an elderly person I thought might be down to his or her last few dollars. In a few instances one of them might look so sad and destitute I'd open the back door and say the ride was on me and end up eating the cost myself for a few kind words in return.

My car was a Checker, one of those big, extra-roomy four door vehicles manufactured in Michigan. The model that, three years later, Robert De Niro as Travis Bickle was seen driving in *Taxi Driver*. Not long after the movie came out I sat in an old, worn seat in Harvard Square Cinema awed at the skill and imagination of Bickle's creator. He, Scorcese, was talking to me and I assumed lots of other buzzed-up drivers spending long, lonely nights taking strange folks to places they might not feel comfortable being in very long. To this day I still feel an irrational identification with Bickle ("You make the move. It's your move.") and wonder whatever happened to the draft of the story about a cab driver titled "Time and Distance" I'd written around then?

Time and distance. Those were the two settings on the old meters with the iron flag that was dropped at the start of each new fare: set to distance it ticked off the ten cents for each eighth mile traveled; set to time it ticked off a similar amount for each minute that went by as you were stalled in traffic or waiting for your fare to run an errand. Setting the meter to time and distance while the taxi was moving was illegal, though unscrupulous drivers might take advantage of unsuspecting riders. I admit I did it often as I could, though never to someone I was sure was on a fixed income or that I knew or knew of. I did have a penchant to stiff demanding out-of-town businessmen I assumed were on company expense accounts and in a hurry to get to the commuter rail station or back to their hotel up along Route 128 or downtown Boston. I did it to others whom I decided deserved it or I just didn't like. Only a few times did someone mention they knew I was overcharging them. Only once did someone call the office to report me to Chuck, the dispatcher.

Presumably because I was the owner's cousin, a cousin he liked and favored, you would think that might have guaranteed me one or two extra better paying fares a day. Nah uh. Not while Chuck was taking the calls and doling them out.

A grouchy ex high school offensive lineman, Chuck had worked for Joey for years, maybe even from the start, and no way he was going to give the summer help, not even Joey's blood relative, special treatment. Not when there were men riding the streets with families to support (at that time all of Red Cab's drivers were men). Not when Big Mike, a feared and uncommunicative man who had been driving a taxi since he was old enough to have a license, might be out there waiting for his number to be called.

Big Mike was on the streets twelve hours a day six days a week. I don't know what kind of life he had outside of that, and it's likely I never let my imagination wander too deeply into it, but his stature at Red Cab was such that he wasn't afraid to key the mic and snap something at Chuck if he felt he was getting slighted in the distribution of good-paying fares. Big Mike always looked like he was getting slighted and that made him a little scary to be around. I don't think I had a single conversation with him. In fact, I don't think we ever exchanged any words at all, not even hellos at Joey's garage where we picked up and dropped off our cabs.

The taxi business attracted a lot of those types, loners, social misfits, those in transition from job to job or place to place or life to life, people like me in need of some quick money, or those others who, for whatever reasons, thought spending a good chunk of the day alone in a car, sitting in stalled traffic and waiting for lights to change would be an all right job. ("All my life needed was a sense of someplace to go," was how Bickle put it.) While the seeming freedom of being your own boss and making your own hours, as many or few as you wanted, of hearing the meter click and imagining a steady flow of greenbacks coming your way, might be seductive, its reality was anything but freedom and riches. The constant hustle to make decent cash, the meager tips, whiney people and empty, frustrating downtime, wasn't for everyone. Joey had a core group of steady drivers, but otherwise the turnover rate was quite high, and he, Joey, was constantly looking for people he thought might stay with him a while.

84 was my handle, the number Chuck used to communicate with me over the two-way radio, as in "84 there's a pickup waiting on the corner of Crescent and Moody." Everyone had a number (Big Mike's was 1) but Chuck never used it to address them as he did me when I was in the office or on those occasions I went out with them for beers and some pool playing. It was as if I didn't have a first or last name or that we had entered a time when the use of birth names was

unnecessary. Truth was, I think he was intimidated by a college kid. Sports and women were the two dominant topics among the drivers, and ones I wasn't averse to delving into great detail about, but books, academic knowledge, those were for the Brandesians, as we townies referred to the Brandeis University students who lived up on the hill on South Street and had long hair and went to protests and who also, we were certain, screwed each other like bunnies on amphetamines. Chuck knew I read books during those dead zones in the mid-mornings and mid-afternoons when business was slow. I'd locate a shady spot to park my Checker and take out the volume I'd brought along, and when Chuck was in a joking mood, or a frustrated one, and there were plenty more of those, he might tell me to put it down and head to such and such a number on Upland Road or Weston Street or over to the main entrance of Polaroid: "I hate to interrupt study period 84, but you need to get right on that." I'd finish the paragraph I was on and key the mic and repeat the address for him. In the office at end of one day I remember Chuck looking at the big, thick book in my hand and wondering just why the fuck would I (I as 84) want to read something that was titled *Cancer Ward*?

I still don't think it's an unreasonable question.

EULOGY FOR THE BOMB

The email that arrived in my In Box on the morning of January 9th brought news of the death of Thomas M, a.k.a. The Bomb. Reading it, the flood of images of him playing hoop on the asphalt court in our eastern Massachusetts hometown was immediate. I smiled at the thought of the five-ten floppy-haired Bomb dribbling in a kind of sideways crouch, his butt leading the way and his torso protecting the ball from hands that might desire it for themselves. I felt the heat of a blazing July sun and saw The Bomb lift off the ground in his white Cons with the pumpkin cocked over his right shoulder in a demonstration of perfect athletic balance and control. I silently applauded the quick flick of the wrist, the high arc and the ho-hum look in The Bomb's steely eyes after another sweet sfooshing snap of the net.

Then I remembered something The Bomb said one sultry summer afternoon when a few thousand games later it seemed we blinked our eyes to discover we were twenty-one. I have no idea what had preceded it, or if it was extemporaneous input, but he sent it out there and it stuck: "You're only allowed so many baskets in a lifetime."

It was a prescient and profound declarative statement and I wondered about The Bomb's last bucket? If it came during a winter league game when he was forty-one or forty-two and long past his best days? The Bomb now relegated to one of those hack leagues we used to ridicule, leagues with bad refs played in ratty junior high school gyms; a strained shot he just managed to get off over a younger defender that clunked the front of the rim and barely had enough forward spin on it to roll over the iron and fall through. Maybe those were his only points of the game and later, changing into his civvies in a locker room that stank of stale sweat, he decided his time might be better spent on a Treadmill or Stairmaster.

I saw him raise his eyes and give his head a little shake at the almost unbearable memory of the magic ease he used to pop in five or six baskets in a row just a few years earlier. Long jumpers from deep in the corner or out beyond the top of the key. Soft little hooks down low over taller defenders. Free throws were a reach for the coffee cup. Packing his sneakers and shorts into his gym bag that night I believe he knew there was no avoiding it. In The Bomb's view of the world even he was only allowed so many baskets and after them that was it, he was all done.

Back in those early days The Bomb was known for having certain idiosyncrasies. He'd never play a game on a hoop without a net. He'd never be a skin in a game of shirts against skins. He also had an aversion for formal leagues. The Bomb never played for our high school. He understood his game was incompatible with the control-freak program implemented by the coach, who never warmed up to The Bomb's hectic, run-and-gun style. The hours and hours of drills that were intended to set up a "good" shot in a game situation were a huge snore to The Bomb. When he had the ball he'd look to shoot, and it went in plenty often. And The Bomb knew as well as the rest of us that when it came time to pick sides out on the blacktop you wouldn't choose the lettered boys over him. And if you did, The Bomb would pay you back with a succession of facials while at the same time illuminating the severity of your sin in a mocking voice.

But was that the real Bomb who would try to break you by draining basket after basket while uttering a string of personal insults? I swear that was a contradiction in him because off the court he was quiet, he never bragged, he never offended, he didn't act like a tough guy. He was a kid from a poor family. He was a bad student with a limited vocabulary and range of knowledge. He had an inferiority complex that I think made him feel out of place in most social activities. But on the court, with the rock in his hands, some substitute personality came off the bench and kicked right in. A rush of blood that induced an almost unstoppable onslaught that had him pounding the ball on the asphalt as if he feared it might stick to it and deny him a move to the basket.

I was a teammate on the one organized team The Bomb played on for the Boys Club. We were fourteen and fifteen traveling once or twice a week to Worcester, New Bedford, Lowell, Boston, and other places. Our coach, a twenty-five year old grad student with sandy hair who also drove the team van, named me captain, but in the games I deferred to The Bomb and he applied his dazzling freestyle playground skills with an inexhaustible drive to score points. The result was an average of twenty plus per in games that might end up 51 to 42 or 44 to 38. If assists had been kept I've no doubt I would have led the league on The Bomb's production alone.

I recall one game, a home game in the small gym on Exchange Street, when he filled it up for forty-three points. It was one of the few times I didn't give a second thought to dish and deal the pill to The Bomb on almost every offensive set and suppress my own desire to score. I watched with awe as without the slightest change of demeanor The Bomb bobbed and spun and bumped and sprung in a delirious frenzy that overwhelmed the skinny white boys trying to defend him. Forty-three points seemed like a million to us in those days, a performance worthy of a mention on Sports Center. But at that time there was no Sports Center. Not even a headline to be read on the sports page of *The News Tribune* that might have raved THE BOMB GOES FOR FORTY-THREE, BOYS CLUB ROMPS. After the game, in the locker room with the smell of chlorine, The Bomb was cool about it. We slapped him on the back, impressed and giddy by what we'd witnessed. He smiled, but not a single word came out of him that might be described as conceit. It was as if he too was surprised by his own effort even though we all knew better. He'd had a good night. He'd have others.

And yet in all of that in all those years I don't ever remember dialing The Bomb's number to find out how he was and what he might want to do that night? Off the court I didn't hang out with him much, if ever. When we were eighteen I went to college and The Bomb went to work lumping rubbish barrels for the Department of Public Works. It was a job, I understood without condescension, that suited The Bomb, that he didn't mind going to nor being seen around town hanging off the back of a scarred-gray packer.

One of the last times I saw The Bomb remains quite clear in my memory. I was just home for the summer vacation before my senior year and went to the court that first afternoon. Sure as the roundball's a sphere, The Bomb was there with a questioning look in his eyes that wondered if this was the time I'd come back with a self-important air that would exclude him and compel a defensive response. It wasn't. The hoops had nets on them and there were still some games to play together. Not a lot, but some, before I moved on from South Street for good. But by then The Bomb was a legend and I wasn't and when I thought of him again I was struck frozen by his prophetic words, "You're only allowed so many baskets in a lifetime," knowing all of mine, like his, were already in the past.

R.I.P. Bomb.

THE SOLIDS TRUCK

A few years ago, as I was riding Amtrak back to New York after a family visit up in Massachusetts, Fofo and the solids truck popped into my head in such an urgent way that I went for my pad and pen and began writing notes.

I was eighteen, heading to college the coming September, and that was my second summer working for the City of Waltham's Department of Public Works. There would be one more after it, a stint digging graves, riding mowers and pruning trees in the city-run Mount Feake Cemetery off Prospect Street. Those jobs for the DPW were desired by me and my friends in that they paid well by our modest standards and were difficult to get; I recall only fourteen being available each summer. My good fortune to have one, if you want to look at it that way, and I still do, came by way of an older cousin on the City Council.

I suppose the solids truck was a step up from the year before when I was on rubbish detail. In fact, I liked it a lot better. Rubbish was smelly, rotting, maggot-infested, and often poorly contained, whereas solids comprised the heavier objects the rubbish trucks didn't take. Those included old refrigerators and unneeded tables and torn couches and broken-down water heaters and anything else you can think of that might be found in and around a home; a rusted barbeque from a backyard or a beat-up workbench from a basement.

While the cemetery would turn out to be a relatively cushy gig in comparison, the summer on solids remains my favorite. I liked Fofo and I liked riding around town on the back of the navy-gray truck with heavy metal sides and an open back. I liked waking up early and walking the mile or so from the West End and meeting up with the other men at the garage on Lexington Street with the styrofoam cup of milky coffee I bought each morning at the deli across the street. I liked the giant effort it took to pick up and discard the city's large, expendable items eight hours a day five days a week, and along with that, I liked going home muscle-sore with the accomplishment of having done a lot of hard work. I'd pay serious money to be in the shape I was in back then. I might have weighed a hundred-thirty-five pounds but it was a rippling one-thirty-five that by itself could drag an oven from the curb to the street without much of a struggle and then grab a hold of one side and with Fofo on the other lift it up and slide it onto the back of the flatbed.

Of course, I might be giving myself too much credit in that strenuous process. Fofo was an all-league linebacker at Waltham High School when my father was there and he was still a big, strong man with large arms and a barrel-sized chest. Even in his fifties he remained a powerful presence in his green Dickies uniform. We got to know each other quite well those few months. Fofo was a man of a certain type I was comfortable being around, old school and matter-of-fact. He was like my father in a lot of ways. Like him, he was athletic and loved sports. Like him, he went overseas to fight in a war and had been injured. Also like him, he'd come back from that to settle in the only city he'd ever live in, start a family and hook on to something that would provide for them and him. Public Works jobs in those days were secure, benefits rich and reasonably rewarding for blue collar labor.

A city of fifty-five thousand produces a lot of garbage to heft and pack and it took many rubbish trucks to do that. Maybe eight, I'm not sure. It might have been ten. But only one truck was dedicated to solids and Fofo and I and the driver, a wiry man in his thirties named Robert, were responsible for picking all of it up. After twenty years of that Fofo knew Waltham's streets as well as anyone. He knew every house and building. He seemed to know everyone at every stop, and well enough to have a few words with that inferred the conversation was a continuation of something that had started up a week or weeks earlier. Maybe even years earlier.

When Fofo wasn't chatting up the citizenry he might entertain me with a historical fragment about something we came up to, something he felt I, a future college student, would be interested in: over there a man named Charles Metz may have produced the first motorcycle in America for the Waltham Manufacturing Company; the original buildings of Brandies University, including the medieval-inspired Usen Castle, were originally a medical school (and where, at a younger age, my friends and I went to a biology lab in one of them to see the stillborn babies preserved in giant jars of formaldehyde); the oval track at Bicycle Park once had been the fastest dirt track in the country, and where a world motorcycle speed record was set (and that after a few minutes of research I see was reported in the *The New York Times*).

I admit those ramblings had pretty much zero appeal to me. I was more interested in the bars, restaurants and convenience stores we stopped at to see if there might be something for us to heft and take to the dump, and if there was, depending on how much was there, five or six dollars or even a whopping ten spot would be exchanged for our services, money Fofo, Robert and I split three ways. That was something the rubbish guys also did even if they weren't supposed to; commercial businesses were expected to hire private companies to remove their trash and solids. If I thought anything about it, it seemed little more than a well-deserved perk for the strenuous, sweaty work we were doing.

That I wasn't able to spend summer vacations backpacking or traveling never really bothered me. I never knew anyone who did that. And seeing the way things are now, in 2018, I suppose I was fortunate to have had something to do in the summers between school years that gave me a decent paycheck for those months off. In a time of unpaid "interns" getting "work experience" doing menial tasks in sterile cubicles for highly profitable companies, I'll take the solids truck any time, any year. Though I feel it's safe to say Public Works jobs that let students earn money to save for college are likely gone forever. Where a kid from a lower income household could find out, as I did, what it was like to get up early and go to work and be responsible for something, even something as unglamorous as picking up battered pieces of furniture and burying the dead and filling potholes (which I did on a few afternoons). All that money's dried up, gone missing into other programs and pockets, and I find it ludicrous that solid, if you'll excuse the bad pun, citizens like Fofo are now reviled for making a livable salary with basic benefits they have no choice but to watch get cut little by little until the point will come when they'll be no better off than the teenager taking their order for a burger.

WORDS OF THE DAY

gauche\gohsh\adjective

    1. Lacking social grace, sensitivity, or acuteness; awkward, crude; tactless

If the word fits, wear it. And I wear this one well. A turn in the mirror, I see it sets on me like a fine tailored suit from Brooks Brothers. Ho yeah, you the gauche man! It's all over me. Just ask my wife, Geraldine. A little snicker from her when she comes into my studio and I tell her the WOTD I'm working on. Lacking social grace. Check. Awkward. Check. Crude. Check. I traced the word's origins back to the gaucho, those mythic rough riders of the South American pampas that Borges wrote about in his early stories "Streetcorner Man" and "The Life of Tadeo Isidoro Cruz." Borges liked his gauchos marginal, and ready for anything, a knife fight, a shootout. I suppose there's no doubt gauchos are gauche, insensitive and tactless, thus the logical inference between the two. Most of them anyway; there are always exceptions. Nevertheless, I'm not one of them. The exception, that is. I can see myself riding a horse on the Patagonian grasslands, herding cattle with a lasso or bola, cooking rice and beans and chunks of beef over a campfire. It seems a better way to spend my days than at a desk in a Lower Manhattan office tower. But of course, that's not true. I'm joking about that. And about the relationship between gauche and gaucho. Gaucho doesn't have anything to do with its genealogy. Nothing at all. I digressed again. So back to gauche. Couldn't it also be a noun, as in, a gauche. I'm a gauche. You're a gauche. We are gauches. What school do you think that ditty would be associated with? *We are. Gauches. We are…* One with a tiny enrollment, I'm sure. Maybe one that only accepted gauchos? Where do you go to school? Gauche U. To learn to be a gaucho? For what other reason were you thinking? To be a butler? Now I'm reminded of a long-ago cookout at a big house on the seashore north of Boston. And I mean a big house, twenty, twenty-five rooms, half a dozen bathrooms, yadda yadda. The hosts' son was the husband of a college friend of Geraldine. It was a soft, summer afternoon. Ten or twelve of us sat at a table on the patio eating lobster and clams and corn-on-the-cob, drinking bottles of beer and gin-and-tonics; out ahead the Atlantic Ocean stretched to the horizon. Our hosts were generous, formal, a touch snobby as their son was, and as we were finishing up the son's mother, a woman around sixty years old I figure now, looked over at me and said: "You were very well trained." She was being nice, of course. Complimentary, I knew. Yet I was bemused. Well trained? Did she mean like a poodle or schnauzer? Or like a *homo erectus* who'd just walked out of the State of Nature but was able to manage a knife and fork? I wasn't sure. But it was apparent to everyone there this working class stiff, this Gauche U. grad, was anything but "well trained" in the way she meant it. Which brings me back to the definition and the woman's lack of the social graces she thought she was representative of and assumed I wasn't or was a wannabe of. And what else must have been apparent to everyone at that table was that woman was as gauche as I, though hers was just a different kind of tactlessness.

narcotize\nahr-k*uh*-tahyz\verb

1. To subject to or treat with a narcotic; stupefy.

2. To make dull; stupefy; deaden the awareness of.

You have your go to self treatment. I have mine. Whatever yours is, as long as you and no one else gets hurt, it's fine with me. I understand. You gotta have something to get through these particular days and nights. Mine so happens to be craft beer. That's right, I'm part of the revolution, if by revolution we mean a dramatic and wide-reaching change of a long established order that was imploring to be overthrown. More power to the talented brewmasters. I'm done with those tasteless, fizzy white beers. They're just not for me anymore. Though, BTW, did you notice I didn't say those affordable fizzy white beers you can still get a pint of for three or four dollars? Craft beer out of the keg, not so cheap for we thirsty folks on a budget. And who's not bound to one of those? My disposable income's taken a hit. And not an insignificant hit. Yet I remain a willing patron of those small, pricey brew houses popping up in NYC and elsewhere. Where I go to mingle with other discriminating insurgents to drink beer described as having "a fruity wheat complexity with slightly smoked notes" or "to save to the far end of the night." The pints at the joint two blocks from my house start at eight smackers and from there trend upward to ten and twelve. But they know they have me and their other admirers hooked by the taste buds. So much so they don't even throw us a freebee now and then. The first wasn't for nothing and the last won't be either. That's an effective business model for sure. Hook the customer. Raise the prices. Yet, we craving beer enthusiasts remain undeterred. We justify the cost with the understanding revolutions don't come cheap. Upending an old order for one many times better is a steep undertaking. And like the mortgage, no matter how much it costs room is made in the budget because you can't live without microbrew even if it jeopardizes the cable and phone bills. Whatever has to be cut will be cut in pursuit of another tasty gold medal IPA or lip puckering sour. You want that mellow, stupefying feeling after another humdrum day in the cubicle? After checking out the latest fusillade of tweets from the leader of the land? After hours of intense art making? After a testy conversation with your mother? If that's your wish you'll have to dig deep into your pocket because in this time and place that agreeable, palliative feeling that comes with drinking great craft beer doesn't come cheap.

caseous\KEY-see-uhs\ adjective

1. Of or like cheese.

And you have a cheese free day too. If that's possible. Here out west, traveling in New Mexico, piling some of my favorite Southwestern foods into my mouth, it's a wonder the blood in my veins continues to flow at a pace that lets me get on to the next meal. Enchiladas, burritos, huevos rancheros, tostadas, dishes with basically the same ingredients reconfigured, cheese being the binding agent, the common denominator in all of them, and not the least common denominator. Cheese and more cheese. Bubbling and congealing. Succulent fermented fungus, with a high content of fat and protein. A yellow blob slowing to a standstill in my GI tract. It has me feeling cheesy, not cheap or tacky, though I might also be those, but like a giant coagulating Velveeta melt (to give a nod to the "like cheese" part of the definition). I never forgot the trip I made to Philadelphia a while back, where I stood in line at a famous cheese steak outfit and heard the guy in front of me order a large with extra cheese. Asking for extra cheese on a large Philly cheese steak is like asking for a second freight train to run you over. You're already a goner, it matters not. Of course cheese has other usages. It's also a bit of baseball lingo, as in, "he's throwing some serious cheese out there." In other words, he has a damn good fastball. Though if you throw too much "high inside cheese" the plate umpire might direct a finger toward the dugout and insist you get yourself an early shower. When did that get started anyway? Cheese as moniker for fastball. Could it have been at a time when cheese was scarce? Rare as a 98 mph heater? Hard to believe, I know, since there's so much of it now. Over twenty million metric tons produced worldwide each year. It's put on waffles. Dripping from medium rare hamburgers. Stuffed in the crusts(!) of pizza. I see there's even a recipe for a cream cheese mask for dry skin. All kinds of uses for all kinds of cheeses. Cheddar and gouda and feta and brie. Blue and provolone and limburger and goat. Soft cheese, hard cheese, stinky cheese you may not want to cut in public. Cheese galore. Cheese cheese everywhere and all of it to eat. Yum. Yum.

chary, CHAIR-ee, *adjective*

 1. Wary; cautious.

2.   Not giving or expending freely; sparing.

Since October 5 is my wife Geraldine's birthday it's best not to be chary on this particular day. Better to be incautious, unsparing, profligate. A bit over the top. Not recklessly wasteful, but leaning a tad to the extravagant side of town will do no harm. Will continue the domestic bliss we reside in. Wary with my funds I will not be on a day of this great magnitude. A big bouquet of fresh lilies coming in the door with me will be a good start. But not all of it. Chocolates, of course, will have to make an appearance. And I don't mean one of those 3-packs of bon bons from the corner grocery. I mean a 25 piece selection from Jacques Torres of nutty pralines, pure ganaches and others with exotic spice infusions. A little time with those, some hugs and kisses for sure. Then the main event, the removal of a box hidden behind a bunch of books in my studio with the hand knit sweater from Canadian Sweater Company I know she desires but doesn't want to spend her own money on. Hint. Hint. (Took it this time!) It costs a couple of bucks, as the saying goes. But so what. What's a few President Grants to keep utopia running another year? Seriously. It's a small sum indeed. Eight bills of dead President 18, in fact, before tax and delivery. And while my pen skipped a bit of white space as I was writing that, I've already given in to it, acceptance being Step 1 in recovering from my sparing ways. It's like walking in the rain in that once you stop being cautious, when you finally accept you're going to get soaked, you can just enjoy it. You can skip along in it, sing and dance, kick your way through the puddles. Just have fun. You get home, you stamp your shoes on the mat, you take off your wet clothes and bingo, you're back to being your usual dull self. And this day is much like a rainy day. It's a day to give it up and splash some cash around. To spend freely. It will make me a little lighter in the wallet for sure, but hey, like I said about keeping utopia running, it's not for the chary.

gallivantriloquism\portmanteau of gallivant and ventriloquist\noun

1.The habit or state of wandering from one virtual or imaginary place to another by means of mediated travel anecdotes or experiences of others, without actual contact with the geographies in question.

I suppose being there is two times the fun. Or five times. Even ten. But when it comes to travel, nowadays cyberspace is bringing the mountains, the glaciers, the deserts, the tourist attractions, and detailed street views of the world's largest metropolises to us. Very few places are untouched by it. Very few that can't be seen and read about by typing a few terms in the Google search bar. The virtual tour of Iceland I recently made on my iMac to prepare for an actual trip there was so informative, the amount of information available to access so comprehensive, it was exhaustive. Scrolling through the sites, I couldn't help recalling my first trips abroad with out-of-date guidebooks and handwritten recommendations from friends, and friends of friends, and then touching down onto an amazing land and getting around it just fine. Now Iceland is a small, sparsely populated landmass between Greenland and Norway. It's small also compared to the population density and cultural significance of most other countries I've traveled to. Yet, as I watched videos of geysers blowing steam and had pilots' eye views of small planes cruising over volcanoes, as I checked out photos of a remote thermal bath in the Golden Circle and after that clicked along Reykjavik's streets in 3D, the question continued to come up during those habitual, and often lengthy, surfing stints: did I really want to continue filling my head with images and information to the point the mystery and excitement of exploring a place I'd never been to might be diminished before the car service drove me to JFK to go there? And if not that, then lessened to feel it was a return trip I was making instead of a first visit. More than once during my research I was reminded of the conversation early in Jorge Luis Borges' story "The Aleph," where the narrator abridges the discussion about modern man he was having with an acquaintance named Carlos Argentino. "'I view him,' Argentino said with a certain unaccountable excitement, 'in his inner sanctum, as though in his castle tower, supplied with telephones, telegraphs, phonographs, wireless sets, motion-picture screens, slide projectors, glossaries, timetables...'" At the end of that, the narrator goes on to say that for someone equipped with all of those real travel was unnecessary. The technologies of the 1940s might have been different, but Borges saw them having much the same effect the Internet was having on me. The world wide web was my aleph and I was a gallivantriloquist walking on Vik's black sand beaches and viewing the Vatnajökull glacier from the back window of a room in the Fosshotel Nupar and swimming in the clear, geothermal pool in Kirkjubæjarklaustur and eating a plate of lobster tails in the Fjorubordid restaurant in Stokkseyr. I saw myself on a stool in Mikkeller & Friends decorative space drinking a Hverfisgata Pils. I imagined stepping across the Continental Divide on Leif the Lucky's Bridge on the Reykjanes Peninsula. I waited in line at the red-painted Bæjarins Beztu Pylsur stand in Reykjavik's center to buy one of their famous lamb-based hot dogs smothered with sweet mustard and crisp fried onion. And after filling my head with all that, and much more, what about Iceland would I miss by not going there? Do the simulations of the computer age make actual travel superfluous the way Borges' narrator thought less sophisticated devices did in his time? Now that I'm back in New York I can say for certain I'll take biting into a Bæjarins Beztu lamb dog over a picture of one every day of the week. The real thing *is* many times better.